Sleeping Beauty

This book belongs to:

....

Once upon a time, there lived a king and queen. They were good and wise but they were sad because they had no children. After many years of waiting, they finally had a baby daughter.

The king and queen were very happy and loved their baby princess very much. In celebration of their new daughter the king decided to hold a grand ball at the palace.

He invited everyone in the land: soldiers, farmers, huntsmen, lords and ladies, and the six good fairies who were bringing six special gifts for the princess. "Welcome everyone," he declared.

At the ball, everyone celebrated the birth of the new princess. The good fairies gave the new princess their gifts of kindness, intelligence and beauty, and of song and dance.

As the sixth fairy was
about to give her gift,
the wicked fairy appeared.
"I have my own gift," she
said. "When the princess is
15 years old, she will prick
her finger on a spinning
wheel and she ...

Everyone gasped in shock! The sixth fairy tried to help, as she hadn't yet given her gift. "I can't undo that spell," she said. "But if the princess touches a spinning wheel she will just fall asleep. She could be woken up by a kiss from a prince." The wicked fairy laughed cruelly and then disappeared in a puff of smoke.

"I'll make a new law," said the king. "All of the spinning wheels in the kingdom will be burned. If there are no spinning wheels then my daughter will never be able to prick her finger."

The years passed, and the princess
grew up to be kind, clever, and
beautiful. She could also sing
and dance, just as the good
fairies had granted.

Finally, the day of the princess's 17th birthday arrived, and there was a grand ball to celebrate. Everyone had forgotten about the wicked fairy. But the wicked fairy had not forgotten. She had been waiting for this moment for 17 years.

During the ball, the princess became tired after so much singing and dancing, so she decided to find somewhere to rest. Behind her favourite bench she discovered a little door that she had never seen before. "I wonder where this leads to?" she said.

When she opened the door, she saw an old woman sitting at a spinning wheel. "Come in," said the old woman, "and see what I'm doing."

The princess was curious. She had not seen a spinning wheel before. "I'm spinning," said the old woman, who was really the wicked fairy in disguise. "You can help me by holding this pin."

The princess held out her hand and pricked her finger on the pin. "I feel sleepy," she sighed, and soon she fell into a deep sleep. The spell enchanted the entire palace, and one by one, everyone else in the palace fell asleep too.

The six good fairies had not fallen under the spell, so they carried the sleeping princess and put her to bed. The wicked fairy had disappeared. Nothing moved inside the palace, not even a mouse!

In time, the floors became covered with dust and thick, tall thorns grew, stopping anyone from entering the palace. The good fairies watched over it as everyone slept.

100 years later, a young prince was hunting near the palace. He asked an old man about it. "My grandfather said that it's an enchanted palace with a beautiful princess asleep inside," said the old man. The prince thanked him kindly.

As the prince walked towards the palace, the thorns magically moved apart for him and let him through. "This is strange," he said aloud, as he ran past sleeping guards and through the huge iron doors.

Inside the palace, nothing moved, and it was very quiet and scary.
After searching everywhere, the prince found the sleeping princess.
He thought she was very beautiful and kissed her gently.

She woke up at once and said, "I dreamed that you would come to my rescue." Eventually, everyone in the palace woke up and the king ordered a great party to celebrate.

The six good fairies helped to tidy up and clean the dusty palace using their magic. Very soon the beautiful palace was back to normal and full of life and happiness.

The king thanked the prince for coming to their rescue, and the queen invited him to stay. The next day, the prince asked the princess to marry him. "Yes, of course I will," said the princess. "You have made my dreams come true!"

The next day there was a royal wedding, and everyone in the land agreed it was a wonderful day. There were many happy, smiling guests, including the six good fairies.

This time, the wicked fairy would not ruin a palace celebration, for she had been banished from the kingdom forever. From that day on, the princess and the prince lived happily ever after.